Little Miss Chatterbox

little Miss Chatterbox™

by Roger Hargreaves

Published in the United States of America by Price Stern Sloan, Inc.
360 North La Cienega Boulevard, Los Angeles, California 90048
Printed in the United States of America.
ISBN 0-8431-1479-7

10 9 8

PRICE STERN SLOAN
Los Angeles

Little Miss Chatterbox talked more than a lot.

She talked all the time.

Day in and day out, week after week, month after month, year in and year out!

She never stopped!

She didn't know it, but she even talked in her sleep!

She had a brother.

I bet you can guess what his name was!

Can't you?

That's right!

Mr. Chatterbox!

She looks a bit like him, don't you think?

You should have heard them when they got together!

You couldn't get a word in edgeways.

Or sideways.

Or anyways!

Have you ever heard about somebody being able to talk the hind leg off a donkey?

Well, Mr. Chatterbox could talk both hind legs off a donkey.

And his sister could talk the hind leg off an elephant!

Now, this story is about the time little Miss Chatterbox decided to get herself a job.

Which she did.

In a bank.

In Happyland.

At ten o'clock one Monday morning
Mr. Happy strolled into the
HappyToLendYou Bank in the middle
of Happytown.

He took out his checkbook, wrote
a check, and went to the counter.

Behind the counter, on her first morning
at work, stood little Miss Chatterbox.

She smiled at Mr. Happy.

Mr. Happy smiled back.

''Good morning,'' he said, cheerfully.

''Well,'' said little Miss Chatterbox,
taking a deep breath . . .

BANK

"For the time of year it is a good morning but not as good as the morning we had yesterday and I dare say tomorrow morning will be an even better morning but it's quite a good morning for a Monday morning and . . .

And she went on and on and on until it was time for the bank to close.

Mr. Happy was still standing there, with his mouth open in amazement.

He'd been there for hours!

"And now," continued little Miss Chatterbox, "it's time for the bank to close an time for me to go home so goodbye and nice talking to you and . . ."

And she went home, leaving poor Mr. Happy without any money.

The following morning she was fired!

She got herself another job.

In a restaurant.

The Eatalot!

It was Tuesday morning, and at midday Mr. Greedy walked into the restaurant and sat himself down at his usual corner table.

He always ate there on Tuesdays because that was the day they served extra large portions.

Menu

The waitress came up to take his order.

"What's the soup of the day?" Mr. Greedy asked the waitress.

"Well," said little Miss Chatterbox, for she was the waitress. "The soup of the day is tomato but we also have other soups on the menu such as oxtail and vegetable and chicken and chicken noodle but we have lots of other things to start with such as . . ."

And she went on and on and on.

Until midnight!

Mr. Greedy was still sitting there, listening, in amazement.

He'd been there for twelve hours!

Listening!

''And now,'' continued little Miss Chatterbox, ''it's time for the Eatalot Restaurant to close and for me to go home sc goodbye and nice talking to you and . . .''

And she went home, leaving poor Mr. Greedy feeling rather empty.

The next morning she was fired!

The same thing happened all week long.

On Thursday morning she was fired from her job as an assistant in a hat shop.

Miss Splendid went into the shop to buy herself a new hat, but she couldn't!

"Oh Madam I've just the hat for you and I know you're going to love it because it's pin and pink is your color and it . . . ."

It was all talk, and no hat!

On Friday morning she was fired from her job as a secretary to Mr. Uppity.

Mr. Uppity, incidentally, was the richest man in the world!

I just thought you'd like to know.

But poor Mr. Uppity didn't make any money the day that little Miss Chatterbox was working for him.

Oh no!

"Oh Mr. Uppity I've never worked in an off before and isn't it exciting and would you lik a cup of coffee and are you as rich as everybody says you are and it . . ."

It was all talk and no work!

But, this story has a happy ending because at the very end of that week little Miss Chatterbox managed to find herself a job that suited her down to the ground.

And up to the sky!

That Saturday evening Mr. Chatterbox was at home in Chatterbox Cottage.

Which was where he lived.

Mr. Chatterbox was cross because his watch had stopped and he had arranged to meet little Miss Sunshine at seven o'clock and he had no idea what the time was.

So, he decided to telephone the Speaking Clock to find out what time it was.

He dialed the number.

". . . at the tone the time will be six-twenty-fi
and twenty seconds!"

Little Miss Chatterbox took a deep breath.

BEEP

"At the tone the time will be six-twenty-five
and thirty seconds!"

BEEP

"That's funny," thought Mr. Chatterbox to
himself. "That sounds just like my sister!"